Spring Is a New Beginning

JOAN WALSH ANGLUND

Spring

Is

a

New

Beginning

HARCOURT, BRACE & WORLD, INC., NEW YORK

BY JOAN WALSH ANGLUND

A Friend Is Someone Who Likes You

The Brave Cowboy

Look Out the Window

Love Is a Special Way of Feeling

In a Pumpkin Shell

Cowboy and His Friend

Christmas Is a Time of Giving

Nibble Nibble Mousekin

Spring Is a New Beginning

Cowboy's Secret Life

The Joan Walsh Anglund Sampler

A Pocketful of Proverbs

Childhood Is a Time of Innocence

for all my aunts and uncles

astrid
blanche
emmett
james
jerome
marguerite
robert
ruth
veronica
willis
woodrow

Spring is a new beginning. . . .

It is a season of young life . . .
of nesting birds
and crocuses.

Yellow is its color . . .
    the warm yellow of the sun . . .
    of the bright buttercup
    and the daffodil.

Then all the world is leafy-tipped and new.

Then the earth is rich with seedlings.

Then come delicious days
        of hunting wild strawberries . . .
        of picking violets and forget-me-nots . . .

and dipping eggs

and finding hidden bunnies.

This is the season of the tadpole
and the duckling . . .

of robins' eggs
cupped in a soft bed of straw . . .

of calves

trying out their wobbly legs . . .

and of the fawn's
first brown-eyed look at spring.

Then new life presses out
from every growing thing . . .
fulfilling our trust,
renewing our faith
that this has always been,
that this will be again. . . .

Spring brings an end to winter
and a fresh beginning.

It is a gentle farewell
to yesterday
and the birth of new hope.